# Illustrations by Jim Davis

ISBN 0-89954-733-8

 **Antioch Publishing Company**
Yellow Springs, Ohio 45387

Garfield was so excited about his birthday that he almost didn't mind waking up.

"Okay, Birthday," he said, peeking out from under his blanket. "I've been waiting a whole year for you. This had better be good."

Garfield started to imagine all the fun he would have that day. There would surely be a big party for him, with lots of gifts and cake and ice cream and lasagna and more gifts and more lasagna!

This is going to be a big day, he thought. I'd better start off with a nap.

And he pulled the blanket back over his head.

Hours later Garfield awoke again. He waited in bed for Jon, his owner, to bring him a special birthday breakfast. But Jon never came. So Garfield went looking for him.

Jon wasn't fixing breakfast. Jon was still asleep!

"I want my birthday breakfast," said Garfield, tugging Jon's arm. "Mmmmph," replied Jon.

"My special breakfast -- I want it," said Garfield, poking Jon's shoulder. "Mmmmph," replied Jon.

"BIRTHDAY BREAKFAST! NOW!" said Garfield, jumping up and down on Jon's face. "GO AWAY, GARFIELD!" said Jon, hiding under his pillow.

This is no way to start a birthday, thought Garfield. He stomped off.

Garfield found Odie the dog chewing on an old bone.

"Hey, Odie, old pal," said Garfield. "You must have something special for me."

As usual, Odie looked confused. Then suddenly he snatched up the old bone and dropped it on Garfield's feet.

"Yuck!" said Garfield. "You really shouldn't have. Maybe you could just bark 'Happy Birthday'."

Odie stood there with his eyes bulging and his tongue hanging out.

"Do something, Dog Breath," said Garfield.

"SLUUUURP!" Odie gave Garfield a big lick.

Garfield decided that getting slobbered on by Odie was not his idea of birthday fun.

Garfield lay with his chin on the floor, so depressed he couldn't even think about food. He was having a terrible birthday. What could make it worse?

A visit from Nermal, the world's cutest kitten!

"You're looking especially flabby today," said Nermal.

"Know what today is?" asked Garfield.

"It's my day to bug you by acting cute," said Nermal. ·

"Too bad you can't stay," said Garfield. He pounced on the surprised kitten, rolled him into a ball, and tossed him out an open window.

At least *that* was fun, thought Garfield.

Garfield went outside to find Arlene. Surely she would remember his birthday. After all, she was almost his girlfriend.

He found Arlene sunning on a windowsill.

"Here I am," said Garfield, "ready for my present!"

"What present?" said Arlene.

"Don't you remember?" said Garfield. "Today is a very important day!"

Arlene jumped up. "I nearly forgot! The market puts out fresh garbage today! Care to join me for lunch?"

"I'd rather eat cake and ice cream," said Garfield.

"Then you'll have to wait for somebody's birthday," said Arlene, bounding away.

In the park the air smelled so fresh and the sun shone so warm that Garfield started to feel a little better. He was just about to stretch out on the grass when a large dog with long teeth trotted up to him.

"Guess what?" said the dog. "Today's my birthday."

"Big deal," said Garfield.

"Know what I like to do on my birthday?" asked the dog.

"Chase parked cars?" said Garfield.

"Chase fat cats!" said the dog.

Garfield raced away, with the dog snapping at his heels. Garfield knew this was his worst birthday. He hoped it wouldn't be his last!

Garfield finally escaped the ferocious dog, but only by climbing up a tree.  Unfortunately, he did not know how to climb *down*.

I might as well spend my birthday in this tree, thought Garfield.  Nobody down there cares about me anyway.  I'll just stay up here forever.  Maybe some birds will bring me my dinner.  Or *be* my dinner.

Later, dark clouds slid across the sun and the wind began to shake the branches of the tree.  Soon it was pouring rain.  Poor Garfield was soaked!

"I could really be depressed about this," Garfield said.  "But I'm too busy being miserable."

By the time the rain stopped, Garfield was very hungry. He tried chewing a leaf. "Bleah!" he said. "How can bugs eat this stuff? I'd send out for pizza."

He had to get out of the tree. Maybe he could jump? It didn't look very high. And cats always land on their feet.

As he thought about it, he edged toward the end of the branch. Suddenly , "CRAAACK!" The branch broke off!

"POOOMP!" Garfield hit the ground. He did land on his feet. He also landed on his tummy, his tail, and his face!

"What a dumb birthday," he said, dragging himself home.

"Your dinner's ready, Garfield," said Jon, when Garfield returned. Garfield perked up. Maybe now Jon would surprise him with a birthday treat!

But it was only a plain slice of raisin bread! "Gee, my all-time *un*favorite," said Garfield. But he ate it, of course.

Garfield didn't give up. After dinner he put on a party hat and danced in front of Jon. He blew a party horn. He threw confetti. "Get the hint?" Garfield said.

"Garfield, you're blocking the TV," said Jon.

"What does a cat have to do to get a birthday around here?" said Garfield.

"It's not over yet," Garfield told Pooky, his teddy bear. "If they remember before midnight, they can still save this from being the worst birthday ever."

Pooky, always a good listener, stared sadly at Garfield. "Bet *you* remembered my birthday, didn't you, Pooky," said Garfield. Pooky seemed to agree. "Bet you'd like to give me a birthday hug," said Garfield, hugging Pooky. "Thanks, Pooky," said Garfield.

Garfield and Pooky watched the clock. Finally, it was midnight.

"That's it," said Garfield. "No cake, no party, no presents. This birthday is now an official *disaster*."

Sadly, he headed for bed.

Suddenly someone shouted, "SURPRISE!"

Turning around, Garfield saw Jon, Odie, Nermal, and Arlene, all wearing party hats. They had cake, presents, and a big pan of lasagna.

"HAPPY BIRTHDAY, GARFIELD!"

"You're too late," said Garfield.

"It's midnight," said Arlene. "So?" said Garfield. "So your birthday is *today*," said Arlene. "You had the wrong day!"

Garfield quickly checked the calendar. "Oops," he said. "Silly me."

"ARF!" Odie agreed.

Then Garfield blew out the candle and opened his presents. "You know, Pooky," Garfield said, "this could be the beginning of my best birthday ever!"

The End